Enjoy !!

Farah Rocks

...and so does Zaria!

Susan Muaddi Darraj

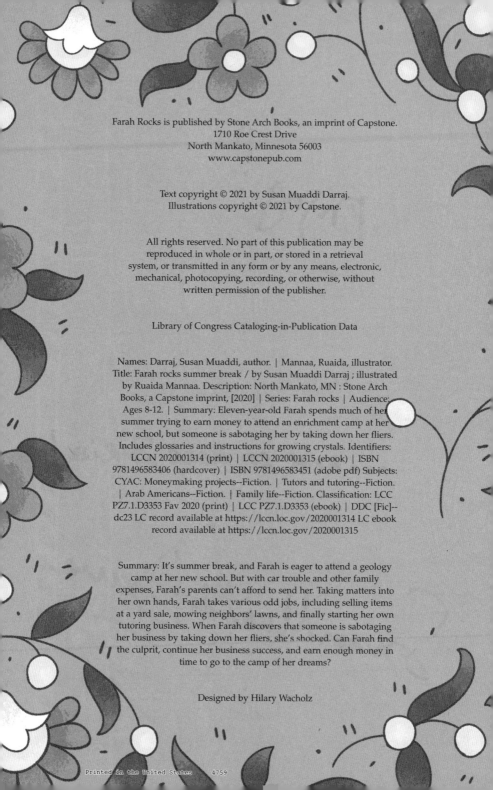

Farah Rocks is published by Stone Arch Books, an imprint of Capstone.
1710 Roe Crest Drive
North Mankato, Minnesota 56003
www.capstonepub.com

Library of Congress Cataloging-in-Publication Data

Names: Darraj, Susan Muaddi, author. | Mannaa, Ruaida, illustrator.
Title: Farah rocks summer break / by Susan Muaddi Darraj ; illustrated
by Ruaida Mannaa. Description: North Mankato, MN : Stone Arch
Books, a Capstone imprint, [2020] | Series: Farah rocks | Audience:
Ages 8-12. | Summary: Eleven-year-old Farah spends much of her
summer trying to earn money to attend an enrichment camp at her
new school, but someone is sabotaging her by taking down her fliers.
Includes glossaries and instructions for growing crystals. Identifiers:
LCCN 2020001314 (print) | LCCN 2020001315 (ebook) | ISBN
9781496583406 (hardcover) | ISBN 9781496583451 (adobe pdf) Subjects:
CYAC: Moneymaking projects--Fiction. | Tutors and tutoring--Fiction.
| Arab Americans--Fiction. | Family life--Fiction. Classification: LCC
PZ7.1.D3353 Fav 2020 (print) | LCC PZ7.1.D3353 (ebook) | DDC [Fic]--
dc23 LC record available at https://lccn.loc.gov/2020001314 LC ebook
record available at https://lccn.loc.gov/2020001315

Summary: It's summer break, and Farah is eager to attend a geology
camp at her new school. But with car trouble and other family
expenses, Farah's parents can't afford to send her. Taking matters into
her own hands, Farah takes various odd jobs, including selling items
at a yard sale, mowing neighbors' lawns, and finally starting her own
tutoring business. When Farah discovers that someone is sabotaging
her business by taking down her fliers, she's shocked. Can Farah find
the culprit, continue her business success, and earn enough money in
time to go to the camp of her dreams?

Designed by Hilary Wacholz

Farah Rocks
Summer Break

BY SUSAN
MUADDI DARRAJ

ILLUSTRATED BY
RUAIDA MANNAA

STONE ARCH BOOKS
a capstone imprint

CHAPTER 1

I see the ball coming in my direction, and I run up close to the net. I leap up and use my fist to slam it over to the other side. The players on my side cheer. But then Enrique, who's on the other team, spikes the ball back. It sails down diagonally, unstoppable, and smacks the ground beside me.

Final point. We've lost the match.

"Nice job!" I tell the other team members, who are shrieking with joy. Enrique grins at me, and I give him a thumbs-up.

Hot and sweaty, everyone walks over to the drink

table. Today was the last day of school, and we are celebrating at Allie Liu's house. She's my Official Best Friend, and her parents invited everyone over for a huge picnic and games.

I head to the creek that runs behind Allie's house. I pull off my sneakers and dip my toes in the water to cool off. Then I sit on the bench under the big maple tree in Allie's backyard. I'm cooler now, but sweat is still dripping off my face. I relax and enjoy the feeling of the grass on my bare feet.

This isn't a typical end-of-year party. This morning, Harbortown Elementary/Middle School held a Fifth Grade Graduation. With the other fifth graders, I walked down the center of the cafetorium, wearing a blue robe with a square hat. The principal called us up on the stage, one by one, and handed us our diplomas. At the end of the ceremony, she asked us all to stand. "Move the tassels on your cap from the right to the left," she said.

She explained that this meant we had officially grad-uated. A *whoop* erupted from the audience.

Holy hummus, I thought. *I'm finally finished with elementary school.*

Even now, I can't believe it. No more lining up for gym class? No more assigned seats at lunch? No more being shushed in the hallway?

Right now, the Lius' yard is jammed with all my friends and their families. They even invited some of our teachers, like Mr. Richie and Ms. Loft.

Mr. Liu and my father are grilling chicken, while our moms hand out ice cream bars. My little brother, Samir, is trying to learn how to jump rope with some other kindergartners.

Just then, a paper airplane whirls in the air above my head, spirals down, and settles on the bench beside me.

Someone laughs.

"Enrique!" I shout.

Enrique LeBrand is one of the nicest kids in school. We've been friends since kindergarten. He approaches me, his arms up like he's just scored a touchdown. "Come on, that was pretty amazing!"

"It really was!" I admit. "There's a little breeze in the air, so that must have helped give the plane some thrust—"

"Hey, turn off your brain!" He snatches the airplane and sits on the grass in front of me. "It's summer vacation, Farah Rocks."

My name is Farah Hajjar, but my friends have been calling me Farah Rocks since basically forever. That's because my last name, *Hajjar*, means "rocks" or "stones" in Arabic.

Enrique is right. I should relax for a minute. We're celebrating more than just the end of fifth grade, after all. A few of us—Allie, Enrique, Lauren, Adaego, and Winston—were accepted to the Magnet Academy. That's a super hard school to get into. We've been hearing for years that kids who go to Magnet end up becoming scientists, astronauts, or engineers.

Enrique hands me the paper airplane. "Open it." He leans back on the grass, puts one leg over the other, and pillows his hands under his head.

I open the flyer and read:

Get ready to be MAGNET-ized!!!

Sign up now for Camp Crystals!

A one-week science camp
to prepare you for the
Magnet Academy.

August 15–19

Camp Crystals focuses on the earth's rocks and minerals.
We will study rock formations, classify rocks,
make sandstone, and—yes!—grow crystals!

MAGNET
ACADEMY

"Wow, this sounds incredible!" I say to Enrique. "Are

you signing up?"

"Nah," he says, squinting up at me because the sun is in his eyes. "My dad is taking me home to Puerto Rico for a vacation."

"For how long?"

"Usually a vacation means the whole summer," he says, smiling. "But talk to Ms. Loft about who might be going. She's the one who gave me the flyer."

"Did I hear my name?"

We both look up to see Ms. Loft walking toward us. She's wearing a loose-fitting shirt with a dark patch on the sleeve. Ms. Loft had a baby almost a year ago. That kid leaves food stains on her clothes all the time.

"I have a flyer for you too, Farah," she says, sitting beside me and waving a paper. "I hope you can attend Camp Crystals. It's two weeks before you'll start sixth grade at the Magnet Academy."

"Oh, definitely!" I respond. "You know I love all kinds of rocks and minerals. Maybe I can bring in my collection to show—"

She laughs and pats my shoulder. "Somehow I knew

this would be right for you." She glances at Enrique and says, "Hey, the other kids are starting a badminton game. Why don't you go join them?"

"I don't play badminton," he says.

"There's a sport you *don't* play?" I ask. Enrique plays every sport: basketball, baseball, soccer, and football. His father puts a lot of pressure on him. He wants Enrique to get a college scholarship.

"Well . . . they're serving chocolate ice cream over there," Ms. Loft says.

"I don't do chocolate," Enrique says.

"They have other flavors."

"I don't like ice cream in general."

"Enrique," she says with a sigh. "I'd like to speak to Farah in private."

"Oh wow," he says, pretending to be hurt while I snicker. He stands up and walks away, muttering in a joking way, "All you had to do was ask nicely!"

Ms. Loft turns to me, and I stop chuckling. She looks as serious as a trip to the doctor.

"Farah," she says, "Camp Crystals is very expensive. I know your family situation."

What she's trying to say nicely, in her own way, is that my family is basically poor.

Everyone knows my parents work a lot. Still, we don't have much money. Part of the problem is that Samir was born three months early. Because of that, he has tons of health bills. They eat up our spare money the way Samir gobbles M&Ms when Mama is not paying attention.

"But," Ms. Loft continues, "I can get you a partial scholarship. The PTA at Harbortown usually helps out with the funding."

"How much can they give me?" I ask.

She points to Mr. Richie, who was my math teacher last year. He's chatting with my baba by the grill. "Mr. Richie and I nominated you. The PTA already said they'd give you four hundred dollars."

"Oh, that's super!" I raise my hands above my head in delight. "Four hundred bucks!"

"Well, that's only forty percent of the cost."

"Forty percent?" I ask, my hands sinking down to my lap. "That means . . . the camp costs . . ." I look at the flyer, but there are no numbers there.

"One thousand dollars," she says in a sad voice. Then she adds, "Plus about twenty-five dollars for fees."

"So then I would still need . . ."

"Six hundred dollars," she says.

"No," I correct her. "Six hundred and *twenty-five* dollars."

I carefully fold Enrique's paper back up into a plane, then launch it into the air.

It does another curlicue in the wind and lands at my feet.

Six hundred and twenty-five bucks.

Holy hummus.

CHAPTER 2

"Six hundred and twenty-five dollars?" Mama shrieks in surprise.

It's the first day of summer vacation. Mama has just finished mopping the floor. "We have to start the season with a clean house," she told us this morning.

She's a little obsessed with cleaning, if you ask me. I am dusting. Samir is supposed to be sweeping the kitchen floor, but he stopped when Mama raised her voice.

Honestly, it takes a *lot* to make her yell. Like when I fell off the back deck and almost broke my arm. That time, her voice exploded out of fear.

Now she stands in the living room, her hands on her hips. Her mouth is wide open in shock.

I knew this wasn't a good idea. It probably shocked her when I casually said, "Hey, do you have an extra six hundred and twenty-five dollars? I'd like to go to a cool summer camp at Magnet."

"Look," I say, putting my hands out to the side, "I'm just *asking*."

"Farah, I would love to say yes." She sighs. "We just don't have the money."

"No problem!" I say. I force my lips to clamp shut and lift up in a smile. I hope it doesn't look too fake, like the way clowns paint weird smiles on their faces. But it's the best I can do.

Samir stares at me, his eyes big and concerned.

I wink at him.

"I'm not dying to go or anything," I say and move the dust rag along the coffee table.

Mama gives me a funny look like she doesn't believe me.

I knew what the answer would be, right? I wonder as I dust. *So why do I feel so disappointed? Why do I feel like someone just snatched a piece of candy right out of my hand?*

I turn to the old desk that sits under the big window in our living room and wipe the surface. We found this desk one Friday afternoon outside someone's house. There we were, just driving to the park, and we saw it on the sidewalk. A perfect desk, with just a few scratches. Abandoned, ready for trash collection the next morning.

Baba called his friend Majeed, who owns a pickup truck. "Quick, quick!" Baba told him. Within an hour, they'd lifted the desk into Majeed's truck and brought it home. Mama cleaned it really well. Baba even painted it with a fresh coat of varnish.

But as I dust it, a sudden, unhappy thought slips into my mind. It's a great desk, but we only have it because someone else decided it was trash.

Mama interrupts my pity party. "I'll talk to Baba when he gets home," she says. "Maybe we can make it work."

"Don't worry about it!" I say again in a cheerful voice.

After cleaning, there's still half an hour before Baba comes home. Samir and I go play in the backyard.

"Want to jump wope?" he asks me. Being born too early left Samir with a lot of challenges. One of them is that he has speech problems, but they are getting better. Right now, the only letter he can't pronounce is R.

I shrug. "I guess."

"How about kickball?" he asks.

"Okay," I say. "Whatever you want. I don't care."

"Come on, Faw-wah," he says sadly.

My attitude stinks, I realize. I am upset, but that doesn't mean Samir needs to feel bad. It's like when one person in class does something wrong and everyone has to miss recess.

"Want to polish my rocks?" I ask.

He nods happily.

I hurry inside to get my rock polishing kit from my room. The "kit" is really just a plastic box with some liquid soap, a rag, and an old toothbrush. I add soap to the box, then fill it up with water until it's bubbly and frothy. Meanwhile, Samir grabs my rock collection from the bottom shelf of my small bookcase.

I keep my rocks in two old cookie tins. I started collecting the rocks back in first grade. Most are rocks I found myself. Others are ones that Baba found while working in the quarry.

Here are my top five most special rocks:

1. A geode that Allie gave me for my birthday one year
2. A chunk of quartz that my second-grade science teacher let me have
3. A hunk of red stone that Baba dug up in the quarry
4. Limestone that Winston Suarez found in his grandmother's backyard when they were digging to build a pool
5. A smooth, rounded tiger eye stone that my fifth-grade math teacher, Mr. Richie, gave me when I got accepted to the Magnet Academy

"This one is gwoss," Samir says, picking up a hunk of black stone that is caked in dirt. I found it last week at the park.

"I'll clean it," I say. I trade him a flat rock that's just dusty, one that I found in our yard.

We work quietly, scrubbing the rocks till they shine. But the whole time, I can tell my brother wants to ask me something.

"Faw-wah, why do you want to go to the camp?" he finally asks.

"It'd be a lot of fun for me," I say. "Imagine if there was a Tommy Turtle camp." Tommy Turtle is his favorite cartoon character.

"I would love that!" Samir says.

"That's how I feel," I tell him. I dig my rag into a crevice in the rock.

"I have thwee bucks," he says, "and six pennies." He smiles at me. "You can have them, Faw-wah."

So now there are two opposite things happening inside of my heart. Number 1: I am still disappointed.

But Number 2: I want to cry from happiness because I have a great brother.

Before I can respond, we hear a weird noise in the driveway. It sounds like a giant is crunching pebbles between its teeth.

And it's getting closer.

CHAPTER 3

Samir and I run to the front of our house. I half-expect to see the Cyclops on our lawn, crunching someone's mailbox in its jaws or noisily devouring the neighbor's fence.

Instead, we watch Baba slowly driving our family car—a rusty little Toyota—into the driveway. Baba shuts off the engine, looking relieved but also frustrated. When he steps out of the car, we say hi. But instead of coming over to kiss us as usual, he pops open the hood. "Hello, habibi Samir. Habibti Farah," he calls to us. "Go inside. I'll be right there." And his head disappears underneath the hood.

A few minutes later, while washing our hands in the bathroom sink, we hear Baba step into the hallway.

"Hi, Abdallah," Mama says.

"Hello, my lovely beoble," he says, looking tired. Like Mama, Baba's first language is Arabic. Mama came to the United States when she was my age. Baba arrived when he was twenty-eight years old, so his accent is way thicker than hers. There is no *p* or *v* in Arabic, so Baba usually slips in the letter *b* instead.

It's pretty cute, honestly, especially when he says things like "Balentine's Day." Or "bebberoni bizza."

"What was that noise?" I ask him.

"The car is habing trouble again," he says, glancing at my mother. "Freddy at work had to jump-start it for me today. I'm lucky I made it home."

"Is it the battery?" Mama asks.

"I hobe that's all," he says, "but it's making a weird noise." He walks into the other room to put away his uniform shirt. Mama follows him.

I know she must've told him about Camp Crystals

because when they return, he smiles sadly at me. "So, habibti," he says, putting his arm around my shoulder. "This camb."

"Really, it's okay," I say.

"I wish we could send you, my dear Farah, but it's imbossible right now. Combletely imbossible." He sighs heavily. "You're not upset with your mama and baba?"

"I already forgot about it," I lie.

Here's the thing about my parents: It's really hard to be mad at them. Even when I want brand-name sneakers but all they can afford is a discount brand. Even when I want to buy popcorn and candy at the movie theater, but Mama sneaks baggies of M&Ms and pretzels in her purse instead. My parents work really hard. So being mad doesn't make any sense.

Baba believes me, and we sit down to eat dinner. Mama made lentil soup. I devour it. Mama works part-time, but she always finds a way to make nice dinners for us. Sometimes I help her. The best thing I can make is tabbouleh salad. Baba likes to cook on the weekends.

His favorite thing to make is pancakes and waffles. Sometimes we eat breakfast food for dinner when Baba cooks (not that Samir and I complain about *that*).

While eating our soup, we talk about the weekend.

"I promised to bring hummus for church on Sunday," Mama says. She's talking about St. Jude Orthodox Church. That's where all the Arab Christian families in Harbortown go.

"We should not talk too much about Farah getting into the Magnet Academy while we are there," she adds.

"Why not?" Samir asks.

"Lana Khoury didn't get in," Mama says.

"Wow," I say, shocked. Lana and I used to get along, but not anymore. For a whole year, Lana had been talking about Magnet like she was already going there. I actually feel kind of bad.

"It's very competitive," Mama says. Then she asks what else we want to do this weekend.

"The library is doing its summer reading challenge again," Baba says. "We could go sign them up."

"And there's a community yard sale on Saturday," Mama says. "At the park."

Mama loves yard sales. It's where we get a lot of our stuff, like Samir's Tommy Turtle sneakers and my school backpack. We got the plates we're eating off tonight at a yard sale.

Lana wouldn't be caught dead shopping at a yard sale, I think. Then I put Lana out of my mind. This has already been a bad day without having to think about her.

But then I suddenly have an idea. I keep eating my food. The idea is just a blob in my mind at first. But as I continue my dinner, it grows legs and arms until it finally seems fully formed in my brain. Camp Crystals is in mid-August. Two months away.

"How much does it cost to set up a table at the yard sale?" I ask.

Mama squints at me. "I think you can get a space for just five dollars."

I have eight dollars in a box under my bed.

"Can I get a table? To sell some stuff I don't need anymore?" I ask.

Mama nods slowly. "Sure. That's actually a good idea. I have some things you can put on your table too. You could keep the money from whatever you sell."

"Really?" I was hoping she'd say that.

"Well, if you're going to do all the work," she says, "you should keep all the money."

Baba takes a sip of water. "I have some stuff too, Farah," he says. "I'll go through my tools later tonight."

"And I'll call the hall and reserve a table for you," says Mama. "Are you saving money for something special? You want to buy a new book or something?"

"I'm going to make enough money to go to Camp Crystals," I declare.

"You're going to make six hundred dollars?" Mama asks, astonished.

"No," I correct her. "Six hundred and *twenty-five* dollars."

CHAPTER 4

Sunday morning is when we go to church—or, as Baba calls it, shursh. I sit and listen to Father Alex talk about "treating others as you would want them to treat you." Sounds logical enough.

Lana Khoury is there with her mother. I imagine holding a sign up to Father that says, "Please speak louder so Lana can hear you."

Just because Lana and I are both Palestinian American girls who are in the same grade, people seem to think we should be best friends. Here's why we aren't: Lana thinks she is better than me. Actually, Lana thinks she is better than everyone who is currently alive on Earth.

In first grade, she told everyone that I wear "cheap clothes." Father Alex heard about it and talked to her mother. She had to apologize, but she just pretended to be sorry because Father was standing right there.

Lana, of course, wears very expensive clothes—the kind with logos that I feel I'm supposed to recognize but don't. She has short brown hair that she dyes with electric blue highlights. Mama would never let me do that.

I wonder what Lana would think if she knew I get my clothes from yard sales. Or if she knew I was about to sell stuff at a yard sale? I picture her clapping her hands to her cheeks and screaming in horror, like she's seen a monster coming to eat her fancy purse.

Glancing back at her, I happen to catch her eye. She looks down at my shoes. I am wearing my plain black ballet flats. They are pretty beaten-up, even though I just rubbed some black shoe polish on them last night. In turn I look at her shoes—leather sandals with low heels. On the front, there is a large, round bronze logo of some kind. When I lift my gaze and look her in the eyes again, she smirks.

I subtly point to Father Alex, then to my ear. *Listen up,* I'm signaling her.

She glares at me.

I smile back sweetly and face the front again.

. . .

"I mean, how much money do you think you're going to make?" Allie asks me the morning of the yard sale. She looks doubtful, but because she's my Official Best Friend, she is here to help anyway.

We're on the lawn of the Harbortown Community Center. My Girl Scout troop sometimes meets here, and Samir plays indoor soccer here. Surrounding us are dozens of tables and blankets spread along the sidewalks and on the grass.

The parking lot is jammed with cars. Cars carrying potential customers. There is a line of cars along the street. They all have their turn signals on, trying to pull in. A man in a yellow vest is waving his hands, directing the traffic.

Camp Crystals feels so close I can reach out and touch it.

"Like, how much can you make by three p.m.?" Allie asks again.

"Hopefully six hundred and twenty-five dollars," I say.

She picks up one of Samir's old Tommy Turtle sweatshirts. He let me have it for the sale because it's tight on him now. I've put a sticker on it that says *50 cents*.

"Do you think I have enough stuff to make that much?" I ask Allie.

She looks around at my items and shrugs.

Here are some of the things I have for sale today:

1. Some of Mama's old pots and pans, as well as her spatulas and muffin tin (she got a new one last month)

2. Seven vases (I'm not sure why our family has so many in the first place)

3. A bunch of Baba's tools that he doesn't use anymore, including two cordless drills

4. Tons of books and clothes, including two of my Sunday church dresses

5. An old dollhouse that I got at a yard sale myself and haven't played with in a long time (although I *did* like having it in my room)

6. A blender that Mama doesn't use anymore since she got a food processor

7. FOUR (yes, four) soccer balls, a baseball glove, and a lacrosse stick—all stuff that Enrique gave me to sell. He had to clean out his room and sports stuff before his big trip and said I could keep the money.

8. A giant bin filled with racecars that belong to Allie's brother, Timothy. Mrs. Liu is very happy he is "growing out of the racecar phase" and that she can have her basement back.

"There's some good stuff here!" I say.

"Plus, I'm selling lemonade," Samir chimes in from behind a small folding table. He's set up a pitcher of

water, a thermos filled with ice, and a can of powdered lemonade, as well as paper cups. "Fifty cents each!"

"Good idea," Allie says. "It's going to be hot out today."

The organizer announces the beginning of the yard sale over a megaphone. "Don't forget to buy some food to support the community center, and have fun looking for treasures!" she tells the huge crowd. Her words hit the crowd like a bowling ball, scattering them in different directions like pins.

I watch as old ladies, young moms, groups of teenagers, and others pick through my stuff. My first sale is the Tommy Turtle sweatshirt, bought by a mom for her toddler. And then an older lady says she'll buy a bunch of Mama's pots and pans for twenty-five dollars, but only if I throw in the spatulas for free.

I realize that yard sales include a lot of negotiating.

I've seen my own mother do this. I agree, and she hands me twenty-five dollars, smiling.

By ten, the crowds have thinned out. I have only forty-two dollars in my pocket. Samir has sold six cups of lemonade, for a grand total of three dollars. The can of lemonade mix cost $2.75.

Allie borrowed her mom's cell phone, and she calls home and asks to be picked up. "I'll be right back," she promises. Half an hour later, she returns with a box of her books and old clothes, as well as her pink wooden jewelry box.

"I don't want this stuff anyway," she says, shrugging. She adds it to the pile we have spread out for sale.

The jewelry box sells ten minutes later for four dollars. Then one of Baba's drills sells for ten dollars.

And that's it. By noon, I am hungry, tired, and feeling lousy. I watch an old man look through my books, pick up a few, then put them all down and walk away.

I feel desperate, like someone is pulling Camp Crystals just out of my reach. It's like that Greek myth of King Tantalus, who was starving and surrounded by tons of food he couldn't grasp.

"Sir," I call after the old man. "Were you interested in these books?" I'm about to give him a good deal. Maybe four dollars for the whole stack.

He shakes his head. "I thought about getting them for my granddaughter. . . ."

"Well, I can offer them for—"

"But then I realized I have no clue what she likes to read," he says. With that, he shrugs and moves on.

Camp Crystals collapses before my eyes like a big landslide.

CHAPTER 5

Toward the end of the day, some other people arrive at the yard sale, looking for deals. These are the vultures. I know them well. Sometimes Mama is one of them.

Vultures are shoppers who know people would rather sell their stuff for super cheap than pack it up and take it all home again. So they hunt, swooping in and snatching up good deals.

Well, I think, feeling tired and hot, *I have one for them.*

"Everything is half-price!" I call out loudly.

Suddenly ten people swarm our table.

Samir picks up on my idea. "Lemonade is twenty-five cents!" he bellows.

My dollhouse immediately sells for six dollars. The blender goes for three.

By the time Mama comes to pick us up, I have eighty-six dollars in my pocket. Samir has nine dollars, and there's only a small pile of items left over—mostly books.

We drive Allie home. I'm annoyed that we didn't even make a hundred dollars, especially after being there most of the day in the heat. Getting to Camp Crystals seems like it will be harder than I imagined.

I offer Allie the money for her items, but she refuses.

"Your goal is to go to camp, right?" she asks.

"Yeah."

"My goal is to make sure you get there so I won't be alone!" Allie says.

Just then, the car makes a funny noise. It sounds like a person coughing. Gasping for air, to be more exact.

Mama grips the steering wheel tightly as she pulls

off the road into a parking lot. She parks the car and turns it off, and the noise stops.

We are silent for a second.

"Mama?" asks Samir.

"Let me think," Mama mutters.

I watch her from the back seat. She seems really worried. She tries to start the car, but that noise starts right away. I'm so hot and tired that I snap, "Just call Baba!"

She glares at me in the mirror. "Thank you, Farah. I wish I had thought of that myself. Thank goodness you're here."

Holy hummus.

For Mama to get sarcastic like that . . . well, it takes a lot to push her to that point. But I guess I helped her get there.

She uses her phone to call Baba. I can hear it ring and ring. She tries a few more times. There's no answer. When Baba's at the quarry, he usually wears headphones to muffle the noise of the drills.

Mama then calls Mr. Liu, who answers right away. After she explains, we hear him reassure her. "I'll be right over," he says.

Allie's dad is one of my favorite people. I'll never forget when I was in kinder-garten and he mixed baking soda and vinegar in a bowl in their kitchen. It foamed and caused a mini-eruption. "That's an acid-base reaction," he said, looking proud. I was hooked on science from that point. Mr. Liu is a scientist in real life too.

In a few minutes, Mr. Liu arrives and hurries over to the car. "No worries, no worries," he says calmly, propping the hood open. Standing over the engine, he pokes around for a few minutes. Mr. Liu has thick black hair, which he wears kind of long, so it flops into his eyes.

Finally he says, sounding confused, "You're out of oil."

"But Abdallah just filled it," Mama says. "He checks it every few weeks."

"I know," Mr. Liu says. "I thought he told me that just the other day. Well, it's almost completely empty now." He snaps his fingers. "I think I have some in my car. Hold on."

He gets a quart of engine oil and pours it slowly into the tube in our car's engine. We've all climbed out of the car by now and are watching him.

"You see," he says to me, Samir, and Allie, "the engine has a lot of parts. The oil keeps them running smoothly. If you run out, or the oil gets dirty, it makes the engine work really hard. Too hard. And so it starts grinding."

"That's the noise we keep hearing," Mama says.

"Yep!" He finishes pouring and twists on the cap. Then he asks Mama to start the car.

It starts. No noise.

"Hooway!" Samir shouts. Allie and I clap.

"I will follow you home," Mr. Liu says.

We all pile into the car. Mr. Liu drives behind us until Mama pulls into our driveway.

"Take it to a mechanic," he tells Mama as Allie gets out of our car and climbs into his. "If Abdallah just filled it, there might be a leak somewhere."

"Thank you so much," Mama says, looking exhausted.

CHAPTER 6

Samir insists that I take his nine dollars, so now I have a grand total of ninety-five dollars.

I am still five hundred and thirty dollars away from my goal. I'm also tired and cranky.

Even more, I'm annoyed with myself for thinking I could make all the money I needed at once.

When Baba gets home from work, he has a good idea for me. "Offer to mow beoble's lawns."

"Do you think anyone will hire me?" I ask.

"Why not?" he says. "You're good at it. You mow our lawn."

"I don't know. . . ."

"It's summertime," he adds with a wink. "Everyone's grass is tall and growing fast."

"But they'll hire *me*? I'm just a kid."

"Of course," he says. "Because it means they don't have to do it themselves."

. • .

The next day is Sunday. Day Four of summer. Baba wakes up early to help me. He fills our lawnmower with gasoline.

"Good luck!" he says cheerfully.

I sigh. "Thanks, I guess."

Baba pats my shoulder. "I'm broud of you, by the way. For making a blan, and working for that blan."

So I set out to work toward my plan: mowing lawns to make money for Camp Crystals.

Except that the people who *have* lawns live blocks away. We have a kind-of lawn (half is filled in with rocks and pebbles). Mama says our lawn is "the size of a grape leaf."

So I push the lawnmower toward Allie's neighborhood, and I start knocking on people's doors.

"We have a lawn service," says one lady.

"Oh, thanks, but we own a riding lawnmower," says another. "We cut our own grass in just fifteen minutes."

One older woman finally agrees to let me cut her lawn. "Okay, sure," she says, her voice creaky. "Just let me know when you've finished."

"Great!"

"Want some lemonade or something, hon?" she asks.

"No, ma'am, but thank you," I say, eager to start.

I push the mower, making neat lines, back and forth, back and forth. It's just ten in the morning, but the sun is getting hot. I'm glad Mama insisted I wear a hat and sunscreen.

An hour later, just when I feel like the back of my neck is burning, I finish. I push the mower to the sidewalk and look at my work. The lawn looks trim and clean. Proud of its appearance, I knock on the woman's door.

"Well, thank you," she says, stepping outside and glancing around. "I guess it really needed a cut, didn't it?"

"You're welcome!"

"You want that lemonade now?"

"No, thanks."

"Okay. Well, have a nice day, sweetie," she says.

"Thanks again."

Then she waves goodbye and shuts the door.

Holy hummus.

I just stand there for a second, unsure what to do. Did she forget? *She is kind of old,* I think. But my Teta Maha is old too, and her memory is like a laser.

I knock again.

The lady opens the door.

"Umm . . . you forgot to pay me, ma'am?" I say politely. It comes out like a question.

"Pay you?"

"Yes." I frown at her confusion. "It's fifteen dollars," I state clearly.

"I thought you were just being neighborly," she says, looking shocked. "You didn't mention money." Her eyebrows jam together at the top of her head. "What kind of racket is this?"

Stunned, I don't know what to say. I don't even know what she means by *racket*. I picture myself as a giant tennis racket, slamming balls across a net.

I watch as her confusion changes to something different. Now she just looks annoyed. She peers down at me through her glasses.

"You should have said something first," she says. She turns her back and then returns a second later. "Here's ten dollars. That's all I have. These kids today . . . the gall . . ."

My neck is really burning now, and I'm also feeling irritated. Why would she assume it was a free service? And now I'm short by five dollars.

I knock on a few more houses, and I get the same

responses. They either have a professional service or they cut their own grass.

One more person allows me to cut his lawn. I clearly tell him it will be fifteen dollars, and he agrees. I spend the next hour making neat lines in the grass until his lawn looks like a sheet of lined paper.

He hands me the money and thanks me. "You can come back in two weeks, if you like," he says kindly.

"I'll let you know," I answer wearily.

I trudge toward the sidewalk, where my lawnmower awaits me. At this point, the machine is out of gas. And so am I.

I push it back home and store it in our small shed. Then I go inside, take a shower, and let Mama put aloe vera gel on my neck. I add the twenty-five dollars I earned in five hours to my stash. That brings my total to one hundred and twenty. I still need five hundred and five dollars.

I take a long, long nap. Just before I fall asleep, my last thought is: *I have to find another way.*

. . .

That night, after dinner, I sit at the kitchen table with Samir. We are practicing his sight words. I help him write the whole list of words on index cards with a marker.

"Thank you for helping your brother, Farah," Baba says as he washes the dishes carefully.

"Why are you doing dishes?" I ask, thinking of how Baba breaks them all the time.

"Your mother is going to the library for her book club," he says, smiling. "Don't worry—I will be bery, bery careful."

"So you fixed the car?" I ask.

"For now, yes. I still don't know what the real problem is. But your baba does have some skills with cars. Back in the old country, I used to—"

Just then, a coffee mug slips out of his hand and crashes to the tiled floor. It shatters into approximately a bajillion pieces.

Baba blinks and looks at us helplessly.

Samir and I giggle wildly and, after a second, Baba joins in.

"Tell Mama to buy plastic stuff," Samir suggests, while I fetch the broom.

Baba won't let me sweep up the shards. He's afraid I'll get hurt. I sit down again and watch Samir practice his words. I stack the cards into two piles: words he knows and words he needs to study more.

Samir gets frustrated sometimes by sight words. They're words like *and* and *the* that you see most often when you are reading. Those ones are easy. Some of the harder ones are words like *about*, *should*, and *around*.

He moves quickly through the first pile, reading each one out loud to me. He gets some of the words in the second pile, but he doesn't recognize most of them.

"Good job," I tell him.

"Not *weally*," he mumbles.

"You're reading, Samir! You've got this."

"I'm not *weally* weading yet."

"Sure you are!" I insist.

"No, I'm not. A lot of kids in my class wead awesome but not me." He sighs and goes to the counter, sticking his hand in the bowl of M&Ms that Mama leaves for him sometimes. That's his favorite candy of all time.

I watch Samir shuffle through the cards. I can see the frustration growing in his big brown eyes. How can I help him feel better about reading?

He's so smart, but his learning challenges mean he sometimes has to work harder than other kids. Just writing the words on the card in neat letters is a big deal for Samir. At one point, he had to learn and practice how to hold a pencil. It's more challenging for him than for other kids because he has smaller muscles in his hands. They weren't strong enough for a long time.

I hate that he feels like he's not doing as well as he should. That's when an idea pops into my mind, like the goddess Athena springing from Zeus's brain.

I get yesterday's newspaper from the living room, then find a yellow highlighter in the kitchen "everything drawer." I hand him both.

"Here—let's play a game," I say. "If you find a word you can read, highlight it."

He grabs the marker.

I open to the sports page, where there is an article about the Harbortown Hurricanes, our soccer team.

Samir excitedly scans the article. "Here's one! And here's another one, Faw-wah!" He slides the neon yellow marker across words he recognizes. Before I know it, almost half the page is highlighted in bright yellow.

"Look, Baba!" I say. I hold up the newspaper page to my father. "Samir read so many words on this page."

"Excellent, habibi!" Baba says.

"Pretty soon, he will be able to read the whole newspaper," I say to Baba. Samir seems to glow with pride.

"Your sister is a good teacher, I think," Baba says.

Samir nods. He starts to stack his cards up and secure them with a rubber band. "You should help Ana," he says. "She has to learn these wouds too. It's our summeh homewowk."

Ana has been Samir's friend since they were pre-schoolers. Like Samir, she gets pulled out of class for special speech therapy. She also gets occupational therapy because she has cerebral palsy.

"I can help Ana anytime," I tell him.

"Hew mom got hew a tutah."

"A what?"

"I think a tutor?" Baba pronounces it like TOOT-OOR. "Mrs. Bergman was telling Mama about that at the yard sale. They pay her by the hour."

"She helps Ana with her wouds and with math and stuff like that," says Samir. "Like how you help me."

"How much do they pay the tutor?" I wonder.

Baba shrugs. "I think she told Mama about fifty dollars an hour."

I wish I could do that, I think. *I could pay for Camp Crystals in no time at all.*

CHAPTER 7

The labyrinth is a special place that the Harbortown Library made for our community. It's a maze shaped like a circle, made out of stones that are set into the ground. You start at the outer edge of the circle and wind your way slowly to the center, where there is a bench. That's where Mama and I like to sit and talk.

Our first talk there happened a few months ago. It was after my parents found out that someone at our school had been bullying Samir and me. They also found out I'd been lying to them about it. My lies almost cost me a chance to go to the Magnet Academy. And worst of all, my lies upset my parents and Allie—but we're okay now.

We sit quietly for a little while. Samir is at his speech therapy session, which will last another twenty minutes.

Mama and I like to sneak away whenever we can to enjoy this special spot. The sun shines down on my face, but it's early enough in the day that it's not too hot yet.

We hear a shrill voice calling from a distance. "Salaamu alaykum." We both turn to see Mrs. Khoury and Lana standing at the entrance to the labyrinth.

Nothing separates us but stones that lie flat in the ground like tiles. But it feels like there are walls and walls between us.

Mama takes a deep breath. I hear it, and I almost smile. It's her way of steadying her nerves.

"Wa alaykum al salaam," we both respond politely.

"Why are you out in the sun?" asks Mrs. Khoury. "The library opened at ten."

"We're just getting some fresh air," Mama replies.

Mrs. Khoury is wearing high heels and a skirt with

a sparkly top. On her wrist are gold bracelets that look like shackles.

Lana looks like her mom. She's dressed like she's about to go to a party, not to the library on a Wednesday morning. She wears pink capri jeans that are super tight and a T-shirt with a fancy logo on it. Her hair is pulled up and styled with a sparkly clip.

I picture myself and Mama the way Mrs. Khoury must see us. We're both wearing jeans. Our hair hangs down our backs in long braids. Mama is wearing flip-flops, and I'm wearing sneakers.

"Well, have a good day!" Mrs. Khoury calls cheerily. "We're here to sign up for the summer reading program and to get more books for Lana. She reads for hours a day, you know!"

"Wonderful," Mama says.

"She got accepted to Riverdale Prep," Mrs. Khoury adds. That's a pretty fancy private school here in Harbortown. The tuition is more than . . . well, more than anything I can imagine owning.

"Mabrouk," Mama says.

Lana smirks as she walks away. The front doors of the library slide open and swallow them up.

"She doesn't know I got into Magnet, does she?" I ask.

Mama shrugs. "We wish her the best. Right, Farah?"

"Sure . . . right."

She tilts her head to the side. "Farah?"

"Oh yes. Absolutely!" I say with more gusto.

"That's better."

Several minutes later, we walk hand-in-hand back through the labyrinth to the parking lot. It's almost time to pick up Samir.

I slide into the back seat of the car. Mama turns the key to start it, but all we hear is a metallic clanking.

"Not now," Mama mutters.

She pulls the key out, and we stare at each other in the rearview mirror. I know not to say a word.

After a moment, Mama puts the key back in and gingerly turns it.

Clank. Clank. Clankety-clank.

Ten minutes go by while Mama tries three more times.

Finally, she picks up her cell phone and calls the speech therapist. "I'm having car trouble, and I'll be a little bit late," she explains softly. "No," she says into the phone, "hopefully, not too long. Please tell Samir not to worry."

Then she calls Baba, who reminds her what to do. She puts him on speaker as we both climb out of the car. "Oben the hood. Now look for that small stick with the loob on the end. It's called a dibstick."

I find the dipstick and pull on it. It comes out of the tube like the sword in the stone in the legend of King Arthur.

"Got it," I say.

"Is there oil on it?" Baba asks.

"It's bone dry," I say.

"Okay, that's the broblem. It keebs leaking." He asks Mama if she remembers how to fill the oil tank.

Mama hurries to the trunk and pulls out a quart

bottle of oil. She tells Baba she can do it from here and hangs up.

"You see," she explains to me, "if there is no oil, the engine can't turn over."

"So we just keep putting oil in, right?" I ask.

"No." She sighs. "There is a reason why it keeps losing oil. And fixing *that* problem is the real issue."

And just then, as both of us lean over the engine, Mama holding a quart of oil—that is when Mrs. Khoury and Lana decide they've had enough time at the library.

"Maryam, *what* are you doing, my dear?" Mrs. Khoury asks my mom, looking baffled. With a classy beep, she uses her key fob to unlock the doors of her big white SUV and another button to make the rear trunk open automatically. Lana stashes a bag of books back there and then stands next to her mother.

They both stare at us like they're at the zoo, and we're giant, slithering snakes in a glass cage. We fascinate them. But we also gross them out.

I want to disappear.

"Well, my car is not cooperating today, as you can see," Mama tells her. "We'll be fine in just a minute."

They continue to watch, like they don't believe her.

Mama finishes pouring in the oil, then she caps it and hands it to me. "Trash can, Farah," she says quietly. I trot over to the black bin by the library entrance and slam the quart into the can.

When I approach the car, I hear the hum of the engine working. I wave bye to the Khourys and climb in.

"You still sit in the back seat, Farah?" Lana says through the open window. "Oh man, I've been sitting up front for a whole year."

She laughs as if it's a fun joke between us.

I don't think it's so funny. As we pull away, I start to sink into the back seat. But then I look at Mama, who drives with her chin up and eyes forward, like a warrior.

And I sit up straight too. I'm not going to hide from anyone, especially Lana.

CHAPTER 8

"Oh, but you *have* to go to Camp Crystals," wails Lauren.

I look at her and cringe. I wish her voice weren't so loud. It feels like half the people at Enrique's neighborhood pool swivel their heads to look at us.

It's Day Seven of summer vacation. Enrique's father has let him invite some friends over to their neighborhood pool. Soon they'll be leaving for Puerto Rico until the end of August. A lot of our classmates, especially Enrique's teammates, are throwing themselves off the diving board. Kids are splashing around in the giant pool or eating snowball cones from the snack bar.

Winston, Enrique, Allie, Lauren, Adaego and me—those of us who got accepted to Magnet—are talking about our summer plans.

Everyone, it seems, is going to Camp Crystals, except for Enrique (because he's going to Puerto Rico) and me (because I'm poor).

"Farah, we're going to *grow crystals*," says Winston, who is wearing long pants and a long-sleeved shirt. He has a sun allergy, which is a real thing.

"I know, Winston," I say, trying not to roll my eyes. "It's the name of the camp."

"And we might take a trip to the Smithsonian, in Washington, D.C.!" he adds.

"*She knows*, Winston," say Allie and Enrique together.

Then Allie changes the subject, and we spend the rest of the afternoon playing Marco Polo and eating pizza.

Later, as we're leaving, I wish Enrique a safe trip. He gives me a high-five. "Hope you get to go to summer camp, Farah."

"I'm trying to earn some money," I say. "But I don't think it's going to happen."

"Don't say that."

"It's true. I need too much." I shrug. "I thought about trying to find some younger kids to tutor because tutors can make fifty dollars an hour."

"Whoa!" He leans back like he's been knocked over.

"I know!" I say, nodding. "But I'm not a professional teacher or anything. I'm eleven years old, and my entire experience is helping Samir with his homework."

Enrique's eyebrows furrow together. "You know, my aunt is always saying she wishes there was an older kid around to help my little cousin."

"Talk to me, Enrique," I say.

He explains that his little cousin Esmeralda is in first grade. She doesn't want to sit with her mom to review her homework or practice reading. "My aunt thinks she would pay attention more to an older kid than to her." He looks down at me. "Pretty sure she can't pay you fifty bucks an hour, but she'll pay you something."

He promises to give my home phone number to his aunt.

"Thanks so much!"

"Sure," he says. "Let me know what happens, okay? I'll be wondering."

"I will," I reply.

"Hey, anything you want from Puerto Rico? I'm bringing some postcards for Adaego for her collection and a pandero for Winston."

"Some rocks?" I ask.

He laughs. "Of course. Why did I even bother asking?"

. . .

My plan for making money makes Mama nervous. She isn't too happy with the idea.

"It's a good plan," I tell her. "I'll have my own business."

"Farah, you have to take this seriously. People will pay you good money to do this work," Mama warns me.

"I know."

"You have to prepare. Make sure you are ready to work hard for the full hour," she says.

I nod. *Holy hummus,* I wonder. *Does Mama think I'm planning to play around for an hour?* I feel almost insulted.

It's *very* serious to me. I have a mission. A goal. I'm going to Camp Crystals, no matter what.

So when Enrique's aunt, Ms. Rivera, calls, Mama speaks to her to make sure everything will be okay. The next day, Day Twelve of summer vacation, I have my first session with my student.

Enrique's cousin is Esmeralda. She is in first grade at a different school.

"You're not in Puerto Rico with the rest of the family, I guess," I say to Ms. Rivera, who greets me at the door.

"There are about eight hundred of them there, so I doubt they'll miss me," Ms. Rivera says with a grin.

I enter the house and sit at the kitchen table. Esmeralda comes in, looking like her hair weighs more than she does. It is long and licorice-black, and it hangs in two braids down her back.

"Wow, your hair is even thicker than mine," I blurt out.

Her mom laughs. "It's hard to comb it, that's for sure," she says, "but I don't have the heart to cut it." She explains that she has some phone calls to make for work. "I'll just be in the next room."

Esmeralda is fun and very smart. We mostly just practice her numbers, from zero to twenty, until her mother asks me to challenge her. "They're starting addition next year," she explains.

I use some of her blocks to represent numbers. I make two piles, two blocks in each pile, and then combine them. Then I show her how to write this in number form: $2 + 2 = 4$. She has fun for a while and even starts doing subtraction. She makes a pile with five and then takes away one, and then two more.

When we get to review her sight words, though, Esmeralda has a hard time. "This doesn't make any sense," she whines.

I put down the stack of flash cards. I understand

why Esmeralda's annoyed. Sight words are words that you just have to recognize. They're hard to figure out in the normal way, by just sounding out the letters. Like, *cat* and *bat* and *flat* all have *A*s that sound soft, like "aaaah." But then "what" sounds like a soft *U*. It should be spelled "wut," but that's just my opinion.

Esmeralda is right—it makes no sense. That's why you just have to memorize them.

"Let's keep trying," I tell her, reaching for the first card in the pile.

"I'm tired, Farah," she says, putting her head on the table. I giggle because she does it so dramatically.

Her head pops up, and she squints her eyes. "What's so funny?"

"Sorry, but you just sounded like those ladies in the black-and-white movies." I stand and put my arm across my eyes. "I'm soooo exhaaaausted!" I say in an out-of-breath voice.

She starts to smile, then stops herself. I can see she's pressing her lips together.

So I gasp loudly and pretend to faint on the floor in a sudden *whoosh*.

She bursts into laughter and claps her hands. "Farah, you're funny!"

Ms. Rivera pops her head into the dining room, talking into her headset. "Yes, that timeline sounds good, Bob," she says while she peers at me lying on the floor.

I scramble up, and then an idea strikes me. "Come on, Esmeralda!" I say, grabbing the cards.

"Where are we going?" she asks, standing up.

"Show me your favorite room in the house," I say.

"Okay." She leads me through their house. It is huge, like a mansion, although it's all one level. The family room is where we end up. It has a tall ceiling with a sky-light in it.

"Here!" she announces.

"Okay. We'll go through your flash cards in here," I say.

"Why?"

"Because . . ." I say in a mysterious voice, ". . . of THIS!"

I toss the cards—all fifty of them—up in the air. She shrieks as they float down around us and settle on the beige carpet.

"What are you doing, Farah?" she asks, looking both confused and excited.

"You get one point for each card you pick up," I say.

"Oh! One point?" She lowers herself to her knees and reaches for a card.

"But you can only pick it up if you can say the word on the card," I add.

She looks up at me and grins. "Tricky, Farah!"

"I think you can do it."

She picks up thirty cards at first. Some cards she picks up, scans, but then drops them back to the floor. "That's all I know," she says.

"No problem," I say, and we sit and review the other twenty she didn't know.

I stack the cards again and fling them into the air. This time, she picks up forty-two cards.

71

"You have forty-two points today," I tell her. "Next time, I think you will get all fifty."

"So what do I get for forty-two points?" she asks.

"You get to play outside with me!" I exclaim.

"Yay!"

I hear a chuckle and glance up to see Ms. Rivera standing in the doorway, looking very pleased.

CHAPTER 9

Ms. Rivera recommends me to another friend, who also has a first grader.

Allie's dad tells a neighbor about me too, and I get another "client" that way. I am up to one hundred and eighty dollars.

On Day Twenty-Two of summer vacation, Dr. Sharif, who lives two blocks away and also goes to our church, calls Baba. From Baba's end of the conversation, I can tell he wants me to tutor his son in math.

"Looks like you have a reputation already, Farah," Mama whispers to me as we listen to Baba talk to him. "You've started a little business here."

Baba looks at me and raises his shoulders. He's asking me what I think.

I give him a thumbs-up.

He hands me the phone so I can talk to Dr. Sharif myself.

"We will make blans after shursh on Sunday," Dr. Sharif tells me. I try hard not to giggle because he sounds just like Baba. "And I will let others know too. Does your business have a name?"

"No, but maybe I should think of one," I tell him.

"Every business needs a name that beoble will remember!" says Dr. Sharif.

Before I hang up, I remember Mama's words: "You have to prepare. Make sure you are ready to work hard for the full hour."

Marwan is a rowdy, funny kid with thick black eyebrows, but I don't know him *that* well.

I ask Dr. Sharif about what Marwan learned last year in second grade. I make a note that he did mostly addition and subtraction. In third grade, I know he'll be doing multiplication and division because that's when I learned it.

Then I call Allie. "My tutoring is a real business now," I tell her.

She sounds excited. "We should advertise it!" Allie says. "You can get more customers that way."

We make a plan to get together the following week, and I hang up. I should feel happy that my plan is working out.

Why am I suddenly so nervous, then?

If I mess up somehow with Marwan, Dr. Sharif will know. And it's different with him because he's close friends with my parents. And what if he tells other people too?

I didn't realize there would be so much pressure in having a business.

I think about other times I have been nervous. Sometimes I'd get nervous before a big math exam. Definitely the night before. I used to study and study until I knew I would be okay.

So maybe, I think to myself, I need to study to become a tutor. I had some good ideas with Samir and Esmeralda, but what if I run out?

I get Mama's permission to use the iPad to research. I spend the next two hours on YouTube, watching videos of tips to help children learn. I also find some teacher resource websites with some ready-to-print worksheets.

I organize the worksheets into one of my old school folders, then label the folder  *Tutoring.* I get one of Mama's canvas shopping bags and put the folder in there. I rip out the few used pages of one of my notebooks. On the cover of the notebook, I write, *Tutoring Ideas.*

. . .

At church on Sunday, I see Marwan during line-up for Sunday school class. He's being rowdy and noisy in the hallway. The elementary teacher, Mrs. Fairouz, puts her finger to her lips. She shushes him so roughly that she kind of spits on her own hand. I try not to laugh, and instead I kind of snort. Marwan notices me and snickers.

In the middle-school class, Lana is showing her new blue highlights to her friends. She sees me but does what she usually does—smirks and turns her back.

After class, the kids go out to the main hall, where the adults have their coffee hour. This is where the adults "catch up" with each other. "Catching up" for Arab parents usually means talking about two things: 1. their kids and 2. food.

Dr. Sharif is standing with my parents. "There she is! Al ustazah Farah," he says.

He's basically called me a professor, which makes me giggle. He's like a cartoon character, the way he waves his hands when he talks, like a bird flapping its wings before takeoff. My parents like him because, even though he is a heart surgeon and his house is bigger than the church, he never acts like he's better than anyone else. Dr. Sharif starts going on about how smart I am. He says how lucky Marwan is to have me for a teacher. He is completely exaggerating, but I don't mind.

"What's this?" asks Mrs. Khoury, striding up to us. In my head, I call her the Snow Queen because she walks very stiffly, like she's made of ice. Plus her makeup is usually shimmery like snow.

"Farah here is going to tutor my Marwan over the summer break," Dr. Sharif explains after they all greet her.

"Is that right?" She sounds very surprised. Like, *super* surprised.

I feel annoyed. Why is that a shock?

Then she adds, "I'm sure Marwan doesn't need a tutor. And if he did, Dr. Sharif, surely you could hire a real teacher?"

My parents don't look happy about that comment.

Dr. Sharif says, "Oh, you do not know Marwan. If I told him a teacher is coming to review work with him, he would not cooperate. But when I told him Farah was coming over to do the same thing, he was very excited."

He puts his hands out to the side, as if to say, "See how simple."

"Plus, Farah is excellent in school. She helps her brother all the time," my father explains to Mrs. Khoury. He's smiling, but I can tell it's fake because his lips are pressed together. "She's also an excellent student. Actually, she was just accepted into the Magnet Academy."

"Mabrouk!" Dr. Sharif says, patting my shoulder. "I knew I picked the right person."

"Yes, indeed. Mabrouk," Mrs. Khoury says, but I can tell she doesn't mean it. Then she walks away.

"Abdallah," Mama sputters. "That's . . . that wasn't very nice."

"It's awkward, Abdallah," Dr. Sharif tries to explain to Baba. "You see, her daughter Lana applied. She did not get accepted to Magnet."

"I know," Baba says in a wicked tone. He laughs when Dr. Sharif looks shocked. "Sorry, but sometimes I forget how to be bolite."

CHAPTER 10

Allie comes over one day to help me make a plan. If I can just get a few more students to tutor, perhaps ten sessions a week, I could have enough to go to Camp Crystals.

"I'll ask Timothy if any of his friends have younger brothers and sisters," Allie says as we sit in my room. We are brainstorming ways to get new customers. I'm on the floor, polishing my rocks. She's pacing around my room like a tiger prowling around its cage.

"Yes! That would be great."

"Nah, never mind," she said, waving her hand. "He

would probably demand a percentage of what you make. He's so annoying."

I laugh because Timothy really is annoying.

"Enrique texted Winston from Puerto Rico to ask about everyone. He asked how you were doing," Allie tells me.

"Cool. I hope he's having fun."

We both sigh.

Allie lets herself fall back on my bed, her arms outstretched. She stares up at the ceiling. "I wish your parents could figure out how to just give you the money," she moans. "I mean, it's not really that much. You know?"

I don't answer right away. I feel like my Official Best Friend just slapped me across the cheek.

"It *is* a lot of money," I say in a quiet voice, "for us."

Allie is quiet too. When I look at her, still stretched out on the bed, she's blushing. "I'm sorry," she says. "It came out wrong."

I turn back to my rocks, polishing and thinking.

Usually, Allie and I *never* have awkward moments. But now there is one hanging between us.

Her dad is a scientist, and her mom manages a pharmacy. They don't have to worry about money like we do. Six hundred and twenty-five dollars probably isn't a lot for them.

I'm suddenly angry. I have to work so hard to get something that a lot of kids never doubt they can have.

But guess what? I've always had more responsibility than most other kids. For example, I'm used to having a little brother who needs more help than other kids do. And I do it because I try to be a good big sister.

Suddenly an idea lands in my brain like a bee on a flower. "Big Sister Tutoring," I say aloud, my rock in one hand and my cloth in the other.

"What?" Allie asks.

"That's the name of my business."

"Huh." She sits up on my bed. "It's perfect, Farah Rocks."

"I know!"

"We should make posters or flyers and hang them all over Harbortown," she says excitedly. "And you should ask Ms. Rivera or Dr. Sharif if they would give you a reference if someone calls them."

"Good idea!" I grab my notebook and jot down some notes. "I can make the flyers today. Tomorrow I can walk around town to post them."

"*We* can do that," Allie says. "I'm going to help, you know."

"I don't want you to waste your summer helping me," I say.

She shrugged. "If *you* don't go to Camp Crystals, then *I'm* going to have a terrible time. So . . ." She shrugs as if to say, *end of discussion.*

We handwrite flyers. Allie draws really well, so she makes a cool border. It has books and math problems and school supplies all along the edge. Then I letter in:

Big Sister Tutoring!

Responsible sixth grader
available to review . . .

Math

Science

Language Arts

. . . with your K–3rd grader
this summer!

I put my name and Mama's cell phone number on
the bottom of the flyers.

Allie adds one more line: "References available."

It is a beautiful flyer, but it took us an hour just to make two. I can't stand the thought of making fifty more by hand.

"I think it's time to take some of the money I've earned and put it back into the business," I say to Allie.

"An investment," she says.

"Right." I get my money from the tin box in my closet. "Let's go to the copy store."

We check with our parents, then we head to the copy store three blocks away. Mama is at work, so Samir has to come with us. Allie and I walk while Samir rides his scooter while wearing his Tommy Turtle helmet.

At the copy store, I find out that one color copy costs forty-five cents. A black-and-white copy costs only twenty cents. Allie and I figure out that fifty black-and-white copies would cost ten dollars, plus tax. It hurts a little as I hand the man eleven dollars. But I know this will help my business grow.

Allie has brought the stapler from her father's home

office. After we get the copies, we decide to hang some flyers in the library.

Mrs. Nirmala, the librarian, greets me at the counter. "Hello, Farah! Allie!" She pats my brother on the shoulder. "Hello, Samir, my friend." She has short, stylish hair, and she always wears cool earrings. Today they look like large, silver peacocks. She asks if we're planning to sign up for the summer reading program. "It's not too late! We still have a few weeks left. The main prize is a drawing for a tablet reader."

"I want a tablet," Samir declares excitedly. Then he pauses. "What's a tablet?"

I forgot to sign up this year because I've been so busy planning ways to make money. While Mrs. Nirmala shows Samir her tablet, I register myself and Samir. Allie has already signed up.

The high schooler who volunteers there offers us stickers of Harbortown Library's mascot, the Hound. He's a cute cartoon dog who wears a Sherlock Holmes hat and carries a book under his arm.

"Take as many as you want," he tells us. The stickers are different sizes and colors.

I take a bunch of them, thinking, *I now have prizes for my students.*

Mrs. Nirmala offers to keep a few flyers at the information desk. She shows us the bulletin board where we can hang a copy. I staple the four corners of my small flyer to the board.

We all step back and look at it. It's black and white, like a little piano keyboard in the middle of a busy, colorful cloud of other posters. But it's perfect in its own way.

"Let's go put up the west," says Samir, strapping his helmet back on.

We go to Harbortown Mart and also to the community center. Then we find a spot at the bulletin board in front of the nail salon. And finally we put one on the news wall in Harbortown Pizza and Sub Shop.

"Well, nobody can say they don't know you're available to tutor," says Allie with a grin. "We wallpapered

Harbortown with Big Sister Tutoring. Everyone will know you have a business."

I suddenly feel a huge load of doubt, like an avalanche, knocking down my enthusiasm. What if everyone who sees my little flyer thinks it's silly?

"Would you hire me? Or at least call me, based on the flyer?" I ask Allie.

"Definitely!"

"How about you?" I ask my brother.

"Oh no, not me," he says. He uses his foot to push off the sidewalk, propelling his scooter faster.

"Why not?" Allie and I ask at the same time.

He glances up at us. "Why would I pay you? You're my sistah. You should help me fow fwee."

He gets so annoyed that we are laughing our heads off that he zips by us, daring us to catch him.

CHAPTER 11

I go to Marwan's house several times over the next few weeks. It's nice because I actually get to see Mrs. Sharif. She has lung problems, so she doesn't leave the house too often. She had cancer five years ago and went through a lot of treatments. She doesn't have cancer anymore, but she had to quit her job because she is always tired. She hardly ever comes to church except for the holidays.

I sit with her on her living room couch. She is eating bizir and reading a novel.

"My mother says hello to you," I tell her.

"Thanks, habibti," she says. "What an honor that you got into the Magnet Academy. You must be very excited."

"I am," I say. "I can't wait. The camp I'm saving to go to is part of the school's program too."

"Not many students get accepted." She lowers her voice. "Poor Lana was very upset not to get in."

I hate to think about Lana. Part of me feels sorry for her. I think about how we used to play together when we were little kids. We sat together during Sunday school classes. We played on the playground together. We took dabke lessons together, learning how to do the line dance, stamping our feet in time to the music.

Lana changed toward me when we got older. Things became awkward when she started having birthday parties at fancy places. I always had parties at my house. Mama would make a nice cake, and we'd play outside. But one year, Lana's mother booked a whole beauty salon for Lana's birthday. All the girls who attended got their fingernails and toenails manicured. They even got facials.

She handed out invitations after Sunday school one day in third grade. She didn't hand one to me.

"Sorry, Farah. I can only invite ten girls," she'd

explained, like it was no big deal. Like she wasn't breaking my heart.

Mrs. Sharif gets me out of my thoughts. "I'm so happy that you've been helping Marwan," she says. "He showed me the dice game you created. So smart." She hands me a tray of sesame cookies.

"Thanks," I say, taking a cookie. I got the idea for the dice game from a teacher's website. You roll a pair of dice and multiply the two numbers that are rolled.

"He just doesn't like to sit and study with me or his father. He's doing a better job of listening to you instead of his boring parents."

This, I realize, is something that is really helping my business. I am not their sister, or their teacher, or their parent. I'm an older kid. And to them, older kids are cool.

I wonder if Esmeralda and Marwan know that people in my own grade used to call me a nerd. I'm glad it doesn't matter to them.

Soon, Marwan and I are sitting on the floor, and our books and cards are on the coffee table. Marwan is a fun kid. He has a cute way of tugging on his ears when he's thinking hard about an answer. But it's been half an hour, and he is getting "bouncy," as Mama would say.

"Sit still, Marwan," I tell him. I'm using flash cards to review his multiplication facts. "We just have to go through these a couple more times."

"I already know them!" he moans. He is bouncing up and down like a spring. "We did the dice game."

"You don't know all of them," I say. "We practice our facts in lots of different ways."

"This is boring," he pouts.

His mother looks up from her book with a frown. "Pay attention, Marwan," she says sternly.

I know I have to do something different. I stand up. He watches me as I walk across the room, then lay the cards face-up on the carpet.

"Whatcha doing?" he asks. He stares at me curiously.

I ignore him. I move back, laying more cards face-up.

The problems are staring up at me. The answers are hidden on the back.

"Farah? What are you doing?" he asks again.

I smile at him but still don't answer. I snake a line of cards all the way from the kitchen to the front door.

He watches me silently. Even Mrs. Sharif puts down her novel to see what I am doing. By the time I'm done, the chain of cards on the carpet loops around the room, under the table and around the couch.

"It's a math train," I finally tell him. "Ready to ride?"

"A math . . . *train*?" He jumps up and comes over to where I'm standing.

I explain the rules. "You can only ride the train if you can tell me the answer to the card. If you get stuck, you have to go back."

"And what if I know them all?"

"You get a prize."

Mrs. Sharif is smiling. "How clever," she murmurs.

"Fine!" Marwan walks to the start. He picks up the first card. "Two times four." He snickers. "Easy. Eight!"

"Put it down and go to the next one," I say.

He gets the next three easily. But then he hits eight times seven. He stops and squints at the card as if the answer will suddenly appear on the front.

"Forty-two?" he asks.

"Nope. Back to the start."

He gets it on the third try, but we are out of time.

"But I didn't finish the train!" Marwan says.

"You can ride next time."

Dr. Sharif walks into the room and stares at the line of cards across his carpet. "You're very creative," he says. He hands me a ten-dollar bill. "Very smart girl. I'm going to tell everyone at shursh about you. I bet Mr. Munir will call you about his daughter. She's having trouble with her summer reading assignments."

"Thank you," I say.

"You could also call him yourself," Mrs. Sharif tells me. "Tell him you are available. Your parents have his number."

"Maybe I will."

CHAPTER 12

It's Day Thirty-Three of summer. In three weeks of tutoring, I've made almost two hundred dollars. As Ms. Rivera pays me after my latest tutoring session with Esmeralda, I realize I am just three hundred dollars away from my goal. There is one month left until Camp Crystals.

I wave goodbye to Esmeralda and walk home. I need to visit the library on my way.

Ms. Loft accepted my application for the camp. I had to send her a seventy-five dollar down payment. I gave the cash—three twenties, a ten, and a five—to Mama. She wrote a check and mailed it. I felt very grown-up that I was making my own down payment on the camp. Samir looked at me in awe.

I walk into the library and glance at the bulletin board. But something makes me stop.

My poster is not there. My little black-and-white flyer is gone.

I move even closer. I can see the staples still stuck in the board where I hung it. There is a small triangle of white paper trapped under one of the staples.

Why did Mrs. Nirmala remove it? I wonder. I start to panic. I only have a few more weeks to get as many tutoring sessions as I can.

I hurry inside and find her at the information desk.

"Hello, Farah," she says. "How are—"

"Why did you take down my flyer?" I blurt out.

She looks surprised. And hurt.

"Farah, I didn't touch your flyer," she says.

"But it's gone," I say. I know I sound rude, so I quickly apologize. "I'm sorry. But I'm just confused."

Suddenly I am angry. I've been tutoring for weeks,

assuming that my flyer was up. It makes sense that I haven't been getting many new calls. *How long has it been down?* I wonder.

Mrs. Nirmala heads to the lobby. She pushes her glasses to the top of her head and peers at the board. Then she reaches out to touch the remaining staples.

"Someone must have torn it down," she says. "That's not allowed. Only the library staff can approve things to be put up or removed."

I reach into my bag, but I have no copies. She assures me that she has an extra one at the information desk and will hang it up for me. She stares at me with an odd expression on her face. "Did you put this flyer up in other locations around town?"

"Yes," I reply. "The nail salon, Harbortown Mart . . ." My voice trails off as I start to get her point.

"You might want to check on those," she says in a grim voice.

. • .

Every flyer is gone.

Every single one has been taken down.

I ask the owner of the pizza and sub shop. Then I check with the manager of Harbortown Mart and Mrs. Kim, who owns the nail salon.

They all say the same thing. "We didn't take it down. We don't know who did."

"This is sabotage," Allie proclaims. We are at her house, throwing rocks into the creek. I throw one that skips twice across the water.

"Why would someone take down only my poster?" I wonder out loud. "It's so weird."

"We should ask people to stand guard."

"And do what?"

"Watch out in case the person does it again," says Allie.

"And tackle them to the ground!" I say. We both laugh.

"I can imagine you, Farah Rocks, chasing someone down the street. Just launching yourself at some bad guy with a face mask."

"I could do it too," I reply, flexing my muscles.

"Maybe you can stand at the library," Allie says. "I'll take the supermarket. Winston can watch out at the . . ."

As she continues, I imagine my friends protecting my flyers like a team of bodyguards.

Mrs. Liu feeds us lunch. After, I call Mama to tell her about the posters. She sounds upset that anyone would do that. "Are you sure it's not a mistake?" she asks.

"Seems like it was done on purpose," I reply.

I ask if I can go around with Allie to look for more places to hang my flyers.

"Yes." Her voice is firm. And a little bit angry. "Hang them everywhere you can, habibti."

Allie and I spend the morning replacing all the posters. We go to every store, every restaurant, every public place we can. We tape them to telephone poles. We ask the manager of the gas station if we can tape them to the gas pumps. Surprisingly, he agrees. Father Alex lets me hang one on the community board in our church.

All of Harbortown, it seems, looks like a giant advertisement for Big Sister Tutoring.

But I'm worried that I have already lost a lot of time. "Do you think people are seeing the flyers now?" I ask Allie.

"For sure," she says. "You're going to get tons of calls this week. You'll see."

I do get a few calls. Three of them turn into new customers. Mama doesn't know them, so I am not allowed to go to their homes. Instead we agree to meet at the library. Mrs. Nirmala reserves one of the study rooms for me.

My poster has been taken down one more time, she tells me a week later. Luckily I had left a stack of copies with her. "I put up a new one," she says. "And I also put up a sign of my own."

I look at the board in the lobby. A long strip of paper runs across the top of it. *Only library staff may add or remove signs on this board. Anyone who tampers with it will be banned from the library.*

"Wow, you mean business," I say.

"Oh yes, I sure do," she replies, putting her hands on her hips.

CHAPTER 13

Two more weeks pass by quickly. My flyers are taken down twice more, but Mrs. Nirmala replaces them. So do Mrs. Kim from the nail salon and Mr. Baldelli from Harbortown Pizza and Sub Shop. "I don't know who is doing this," says Mr. Baldelli, "but it's pretty sneaky. And mean."

Mama is concerned about the flyers. One evening, I overhear her talking to Baba in the kitchen. "Who can it be? They are not taking down anything else—just Farah's flyers."

"It's terrible," Baba agrees in Arabic. "I'm worried about it."

"I don't like the idea of someone bothering her like this. Abdallah, do you think we have enough . . . ," she asks hesitantly, ". . . you know? Enough to just give her the rest?"

"I checked already," he says sadly. "I even tried to get more hours at the quarry. It's just too big a sum. And for one week of camp."

"I know," Mama agrees. "And yet, many camps cost even more than that."

"She is wonderful, no?" Baba says. "To be working and making money because she wants to do this camb, no matter what?"

"She is excellent, this girl," Mama agrees. "Nothing can stop her."

I sneak back up to my room, smiling. While I'm up there, I think about what to do. I have just two weeks before I have to pay the balance for Camp Crystals.

I remember what Dr. Sharif said about Mr. Munir from church. I go back downstairs and ask Baba if I can call him.

Baba looks up Mr. Munir's number on his cell phone and hands it to me.

I hit the call button.

"Hi, Mr. Munir. This is Farah Hajjar. Abdallah Hajjar's daughter."

"Hello, young lady." He sounds happy to hear my voice, so that's a good sign. "How can I helb you?"

"I'm calling because Dr. Sharif said you might be interested in tutoring for your daughter. I'm tutoring Marwan now, and I have free time to—"

"Oh, I wish you had called earlier." He sounds sad. "I just hired another tutor last week."

"Oh, okay. No problem. Thanks, anyway."

"You and her should go into business," he says, laughing. "Two are better than one, you know."

"Who?"

"You're friends anyway, aren't you?"

"Who, Mr. Munir?"

"Lana. The Khourys' daughter." He pauses. "She started her own tutoring business this summer as well."

I'm so shocked that it's only after he hangs up that I whisper, "Holy hummus."

. . .

At church on Sunday, I watch Lana walk in with her parents. Only she doesn't just walk. She *strides* in, looking confident as usual.

She sits next to her parents, wearing a sparkly dress with a matching headband. I look down at my old dress. It is very clean and neat, but the skirt is long and baggy. It looks like a little girl's dress. Lana's dress is way more fashionable than mine.

I feel bad about it—for about thirty seconds.

I turn my head and look at my mother. Her skirt and blouse are simple styles, but they look beautiful on her. She's wearing her favorite color, burgundy, which makes her hair and eyes look even darker and prettier.

Then I look at her hands. My mama has hardworking hands. Strong hands. I slip my hand into one of hers. She smiles down at me and kisses the top of my head. As I sit there listening to Father Alex, I get ready for Lana. I'm angry. In my mind, I put the anger on like it's armor.

I find her after Sunday school, standing by the hummus and manaeesh table. Our church's coffee hour takes place after mass, but it's really like a full dinner. You eat more here than you would at a restaurant.

"Lana, I heard you have your own tutoring business," I say.

"Yeah," she says with a sneer. She looks annoyed that I am standing next to her.

"Me too."

"Good for you." She smirks. "Maybe you can use the money to buy some decent clothes."

I pause. If I am a red, bull's-eye target, she just drove an arrow right to my center. And it hurts.

But I think of Mama's hands, and I fire back: "I would make more money if someone would stop their sabotage."

"What's your point?"

"You've been taking down my posters, Lana."

"You're crazy," she says.

I think, for a brief moment, that maybe I am wrong. Maybe I'm being unfair. I don't have any proof that she's been doing it. But I do know that:

- She *does* go to the library regularly because she signed up for the summer program.
- She suddenly started her business after I started mine.
- She hates me because I got into Magnet and she didn't.

I press on, inventing some proof of my own. "You were seen, you know. At the library."

Her eyes widen a little. "You're a liar. I couldn't have been seen because I didn't do anything."

I continue anyway. "There's a camera outside the nail salon. You were caught on video."

She says nothing. Her lips are pressed firmly together.

Victory.

"What I'm saying is, if my flyers keep disappearing, I'm going to report you," I say.

"You're such a brat, Farah Hajjar!" she hisses.

"I'm just trying to make some money. You're the one who is sabotaging me."

"I hope your stupid business fails," she says. She tucks her perfect, blue-dyed hair behind her ear. Then she walks away from me.

"It won't," I mutter.

I find my parents helping clean the tables after coffee hour. I offer to take a full trash bag out to the dumpster behind the church.

"Meet us at the car, Farah," Mama says.

I toss the bag into the tall dumpster and walk back around the building. That's when I hear it—a grinding, clanky, awful noise. It can only be one thing. Our car.

I stand on the sidewalk with Dr. Sharif, Mama,

Samir, and a few other people. Baba is in the car, trying to start it again.

Grind.

Clank.

Then we all hear it at once— a startling *SNAP.*

And with a huff, the car surrenders and dies.

CHAPTER 14

While members of St. Jude Church watch, a tow truck arrives in the parking lot. The driver gets out and talks to Baba. Then he attaches a big chain to the front of our little car, hooking it up to the back of the truck. A few minutes later, the truck leaves the lot, pulling our car behind it.

Samir asks where he's taking our car. He's holding his Tommy Turtle game cards and his book, which were in the back seat. I have my box of rocks, which I play with during car rides, and the graphic novel I checked out from the library.

"To the mechanic," Baba answers. "We will see if our car can be fixed or not."

"I hope so," Mama says.

Dr. Sharif drives us home in his car. Then he plans to return to church to take his own family home. He has a car he's been thinking of selling, he says, now that his wife doesn't really drive anymore. "Let me know if you need to borrow it for a time."

"Thank you!" Baba says. He shakes his hand gratefully.

Later that evening, Baba gets a phone call from Harbortown Mechanics. Right away I can tell the news is bad. I hear him sighing. When he hangs up, he looks at Mama. "We can fix it for three thousand dollars."

She gasps. "Oh no."

Baba slumps on the couch. "I can take the bus to work."

"You'd have to get to the bus stop," she says. "And the L bus doesn't reach your work. You would have to get off somewhere and take the S bus."

"Yes," he says with another sigh.

He calls Dr. Sharif, who agrees to drive the car over

later. When he arrives, he tells Mama and Baba to drive it for a week to see if they like it. "If you do, we will talk."

Baba takes us all out for a drive. First we drop off Dr. Sharif at home. Then we drive around Harbortown. The car is old, but newer than ours. It's a small SUV. Samir and I like that we sit up higher than before. Baba thinks it drives well. Mama likes how spacious the trunk is.

"Ask him how much he wants for it," Mama suggests.

"I'll wait a few days, and then I will," Baba replies. "I hope it's not too much."

"As long as it's less than three thousand dollars," Mama says in a tired voice, "I guess we will have to take it."

"And somehow find the money for it," Baba says under his breath, but Samir and I hear him anyway.

. . .

That week, I have several tutoring sessions. Another student has signed up, a little boy whose parents are friends with Ms. Rivera. I'm glad because the money for camp is due in two weeks. I'm almost there.

Because I made a down payment, a package arrives for me in the mail one day. It's a welcome letter, plus a cool red T-shirt that says *Camp Crystals*.

Baba really likes the SUV. So do Samir and Mama. And I definitely love it. It's way cooler than our old car. If Mama drove me and Samir somewhere in our old car, and we also brought a friend, the three of us would be squeezed like sardines in the back seat.

The SUV can fit seven people. Plus, it's red.

One night I hear Mama and Baba discussing how much they can spend. "We have twelve hundred dollars, maybe," Mama says. I hear a computer clicking, and I know she is looking at their bank account online.

"Okay, I will ask him what he would like for it," Baba says in Arabic. "I can't wait longer. He's given it to us for a week and didn't press me."

"He's too generous," Mama says as Baba dials Dr. Sharif's number.

I listen to them talk and overhear that Dr. Sharif wants two thousand dollars.

"I will think about it and let you know," Baba says into the phone.

He hangs up and turns to Mama. "I guess we cannot do it."

That night, he drives the car back to Dr. Sharif.

Sitting on the front steps polishing my rocks, I watch Baba round the corner and back up our street.

And I realize that he was too proud to accept a ride home from Dr. Sharif. He walked home instead.

CHAPTER 15

"How will your family get around without a car?" Allie asks me the next day.

I shrug. We are walking to the labyrinth together. I have a half hour before a tutoring session at the library. Allie wanted to come so she could check out some books. She plans to find some on the topics we'll be covering at Camp Crystals. We are both wearing the red shirts we received in the mail.

"My dad will take the bus, I guess," I say. "Samir takes a bus to school. And Mama can literally walk to work."

She sighs. "It won't be forever, right? Just until they can save enough to buy a car."

Allie is right. It's exactly what Mama told me and Samir last night. Dr. Sharif's car is not the last car on Earth.

The mechanic is still waiting on our decision. We can save enough to fix the old car. Otherwise we will save enough to buy another car.

"But his cah was awesome," Samir wailed. "The best one."

Mama shrugged and smiled. "Samir," she said, "if we don't get something we want, it might mean something better is coming. Think of it that way."

As Allie and I wind our way through the stone labyrinth, my mind does the same thing.

What if there isn't another car? What if there isn't a better deal? What if we are meant to have Dr. Sharif's car? What if the only thing stopping us is money? I follow the curve of the labyrinth as I think.

I think about the night I overheard my parents

praising me. They were so proud of me for earning money all summer.

I think about how unfair things can be for me. But also how unfair it is for them. It would be really unfair if Baba had to get up even earlier every day to take the bus. It would also be unfair if Mama had to walk to work every day.

At the same moment I reach the inner part of the labyrinth, I think about this: I am a part of this family. I'm not a little kid. I am eleven years old. I know how to solve problems.

And I am about to solve this one too.

"Allie," I tell my Official Best Friend. "I'm sorry. I won't be going to Camp Crystals with you."

. . .

Mama and Baba both say *no* at the same time.

We are at home, in the kitchen. I have placed the money I've earned in front of them.

Mama refuses to touch it. So does Baba.

"This is your money!" Mama says. She looks almost angry. "How could you think we would take it from you?"

"I want you to have it," I say. "It's the best way. I'll get my down payment back. Add it to what you have. Then we will have enough for Dr. Sharif's car."

"We don't need this," Baba says. He looks even angrier than Mama. "This is a broblem for me and your mother to fix." He picks up the stack of bills. Then he stuffs them into the large front pocket on my T-shirt.

"I don't want to go to camp," I say.

"Farah!" they say at the same time.

"I really don't," I insist.

Baba walks up and glares down at me. We are locked in a staring contest for a second. Then he suddenly grins. He scoops me off my feet in a big bear hug.

"You are the sweetest daughter in the uniberse," he says. He kisses my cheek. "Thank you for being so good."

"You're welcome!" I say. He sets me down on my

feet. I look at Mama, whose face is shining and whose eyes are bright with tears.

I remove the money from my pocket and put it back on the counter. "I'll send an email to Ms. Loft. I'll ask for the down payment back. And I'll offer to pay for the T-shirt."

I smile and turn to leave the kitchen.

"Farah," Mama calls softly.

I glance back. She is holding my stack of money out to me.

I look at her, then at Baba.

"You are going to camb," Baba says. "And that is the end of the story."

CHAPTER 16

When I say that I am not going to camp, here's what I mean: *I am not going to camp.* I'm not sure why my parents don't listen to me.

I'm standing in Ms. Loft's office right now.

I called the school earlier. They told me she worked every morning until noon in the summer. I hand her the T-shirt and say, "I can't go to Camp Crystals this summer after all."

She looks so shocked. I feel bad.

"But Farah, you said you were able to raise the money you needed," she says.

"I know. But my parents' car broke down. It's going

to cost three thousand dollars to fix. Or they could buy a new car. Well, not a new-new car, but newer than what we have. Anyway, they could buy *that* for only two thousand." I pause to take a breath. "So, that's why. I can't go to camp and have fun when my parents are worried about a car."

She does what my parents do. She tries to talk me out of it.

But I hand her the shirt. "It's okay," I say. "I'm really fine. I don't want to go anyway."

She gives me the same look Baba gave me in the kitchen last night. The look that says, *I don't believe a word you just said.* But all she says is, "Keep the shirt, Farah."

I thank her. Before I leave, I decide to add one more thing. It's a thought that kept me up pretty late last night, tossing in my bed. "To tell you the truth," I say, "I think if a camp is going to charge a thousand dollars for a week, then they don't really want kids like me there anyway."

She looks at me, shocked. "Oh, Farah—"

"I love anything to do with rocks and crystals. I have grades good enough to get into the Magnet Academy in the first place. But I can't go to this camp because it's too much money. So they're basically saying, 'This is not a camp for kids who deserve it. This is a camp for kids who have money.'" I shrug. Then I put the red shirt on her desk. "I don't really want this shirt. I hope someone else gets the scholarship money. Have a nice day."

"I'm sorry, Farah Rocks," she says.

"It's fine!" I say brightly. "I've already forgotten it."

As I walk home, I let myself cry.

. . .

That night, I tell my parents what I did.

"Mama," I say. "Baba."

They must hear how serious my voice is because they shut off the TV and give me their attention.

"I told Ms. Loft I won't be going to camp," I say. "So you can just take the money I earned tutoring. You can use it to buy the car."

They both sit bolt upright on the couch.

I hold out my hands. "It's too late. Don't try to change it. She already removed me. And I'm pretty sure there's a waiting list. Another student will take my place."

Baba looks horrified. "How could you do this?" His face has turned red. "Why would you do this? This is our job, not yours."

"I want to help," I say quietly.

"Farah, we talked about this when that awful girl was bullying your brother," Mama says firmly. "You kept trying to fix problems on your own when you should have come to us. Now you're doing it again."

"It's just camp!" I say. "It's not like I'm going to starve to death or have to drop out of school."

"A camb you really wanted to attend," Baba says softly.

"Well, like I told you," I say, "I'm not attending. And that's that."

The phone rings. Mama answers it. Looking surprised, she hands it to me. "Lana," she whispers.

"Hello?" I say.

Mama and Baba huddle around me. They're acting like such curious goofballs I almost want to laugh.

"Look, I'm sorry for taking down your flyers. Okay?" Lana says, sounding irritated. "My mom said I have to call you."

"You admitted it to her?" I ask.

"*No,*" she says. "I got caught."

"How?"

She exhales angrily. I imagine she's a fire-breathing dragon, with smoke pouring out of her nose. It almost makes me giggle. "One of the librarians saw me. She called my mom. Now I'm banned from there for the rest of the summer."

"Holy hummus!"

"Really?" She sighs. "You're still saying the hummus thing?"

"Yeah. I like it."

"Whatever," she says. "Well, anyway. Sorry again. I won't be taking down your flyers anymore."

"Okay." I almost want to tell her it doesn't matter any longer. "Thanks, Lana."

CHAPTER 17

Camp is supposed to start on Monday. Allie is heartbroken I'm not attending. She's promised to update me on every single thing they learn.

On Sunday night, Mama makes our big dinner. Tonight it's musakhan, which is chicken with pine nuts and sumac spices. It's so good that I eat three large pieces. Samir finishes two.

"Let's make sure we all get to bed early tonight," Mama says.

"It's summertime," I say. "We're allowed to stay up late in the summer."

That's when I hear a car pulling into our driveway.

"Who's here?" I ask.

"Let's go see," Baba says.

We all hurry to the door.

It's Dr. Sharif. He's waving a set of car keys. "Here you go!" he says. He hands the keys to Mama. "Mabrouk!"

"Allah yebarek feek," Mama and Baba say together.

"It's really ours?" I almost shriek. I'm so happy.

We spend a long time in the car, as if we've never seen it before. As if we didn't spend a whole week driving in it.

I claim the back seat, behind the driver. There is a cool centerpiece that folds down. The centerpiece has two cup holders, which Samir and I think is super fancy.

The car smells great too, and it sparkles. Dr. Sharif says he took it to a garage where they detailed it. "That means they cleaned it really, really good. Make it like new," he explains.

"Let's keep driving around," I suggest after we drop off Dr. Sharif at his home.

"Not tonight," Mama says, laughing. "Besides, you rode around in it all week."

"I know, but it wasn't ours then!" I reply.

"True, but you need to get to bed soon," says Mama.

"It's summer!" I say.

"But you have a big day tomorrow, Farah," Baba says.

"What are you talking about?"

"Farah! I forgot to mention it," Mama says. She tilts her head and gazes back at me. "You're going to Camp Crystals."

. . .

When I wake up the next morning, there is a shirt lying on the chair in my room. My red Camp Crystals shirt.

Baba drives me to camp and explains everything to me. "You are not allowed to give up something so imbortant," he says, "even though I know you were being bery mature and bery resbonsible."

"But how did you pay for the camp?" I ask. "The money was used to buy the car, right?"

He shakes his head. "No. The mechanic agreed to give us money for our old car. He is going to chob it ub for barts."

"Chop it up?" I ask.

He nods. "Yes, they take it abart and use bieces of it for fixing other cars. All we owe Dr. Sharif is a few hundred dollars. He agreed that we could bay him that over the next few months."

"You could have just taken the money I made," I say. In a weird way, I feel hurt that they didn't want my help.

"Or you could just attend the camb since you worked hard for it."

"But I didn't have enough anyway," I say. "That's why I'm so confused."

He tells me that Ms. Loft called him. She explained that the PTA had decided to increase their scholarships to students. Instead of four hundred dollars, they would now pay six hundred. "Farah helped me see that the price tag is like a big *KEEP OUT* sign," she told Baba. She explained to the PTA that kids might feel unwanted at camp because the price was too high.

"So I have enough?" I ask when Baba is done explaining.

"You even have some sbending money left over," he says.

Camp Crystals is being held in the Science Building at the Magnet Academy. We pull up to the sidewalk. There are camp counselors there, wearing red T-shirts and holding clipboards.

A big sign behind them reads:

I open the car door. A young woman says to me, "Hey! Welcome to camp!"

"Thanks!" I say, climbing out. I pull my backpack over my shoulder. "I'm excited to be here."

"What's your name?" she asks, looking at her clipboard.

"Farah Hajjar."

She smiles even wider. "You're Farah Rocks. We've heard all about you!"

Baba laughs in the car. He blows me a kiss. "Enjoy it, habibti!"

TO: Enrique LeBrand (hurricanesfan1@harbormail.com)
FROM: Farah Hajjar (farahrocks@harbormail.com)
SUBJECT: Update from home!

Hey Enrique,

I hope you are having a blast in Puerto Rico! I wanted to tell you that I made enough money to get to Camp Crystals! Thanks for telling your aunt to hire me as a tutor. And for encouraging me in the first place.

Camp has been so much fun. Allie and I made notes on all the experiments so that you can do them too.

Did you remember to get me some rocks from Puerto Rico?

I grew you some crystals, right here in Harbortown. They'll be waiting for you!

See you soon!

Farah Rocks

How to Grow Crystals

At Camp Crystals, Farah and Allie learned how to grow their own crystals. Try it yourself!

You'll be using magnesium sulfate, which is sold in stores as Epsom salt. It's safe to use, so you may only need an adult to help you with getting some hot water.

What You Need:

- ½ cup water
- glass bowl
- microwave
- ¼ cup Epsom salt (magnesium sulfate)
- food coloring

What You Do:

1. Pour the water in the glass bowl.

2. Put it in the microwave for one minute on high so that it boils. Let an adult help you remove it carefully.

3. In the bowl, stir in the Epsom salt until the salt will no longer dissolve. It's okay if you have some undissolved particles at the bottom.

4. Add a couple drops of food coloring if you want your crystals to be colored.

5. Put the bowl in the refrigerator. In a few hours, you should see your solution has generated lots of crystals!

6. You can also put your bowl in a sunny window and watch crystals form as the water evaporates.

Glossary

accent (AK-sent)—a way of pronouncing words, shared by people of a particular region

badminton (BAD-min-tuhn)—a game in which players use rackets to hit a shuttlecock back and forth over a net

cerebral palsy (seh-REE-bruhl PALL-see)— a condition that is caused by damage to the brain around the time of birth

client (KLYE-uhnt)—a customer

Cyclops (SYE-clops)—a giant in Greek mythology with a single eye in the middle of the forehead

down payment (DOUN PAY-mint)—a part of a price paid when something is bought, with an agreement to pay the rest later

negotiate (ni-GOH-shee-ate)—to try to reach an agreement by discussing something

occupational therapy (ahk-yuh-PAY-shuhn-uhl THER-uh-pee)—treatment that helps people with physical or mental problems learn to do the activities of daily life

pandero (pan-DAIR-oh)—a kind of tambourine common in Spain, Latin America, and the Spanish-speaking Caribbean

racket (RAK-it)—a dishonest scheme or business activity

reference (REF-ur-uhns)—a statement about someone's personal abilities or qualities

sabotage (SAB-uh-tahzh)—the deliberate damage of property, especially to stop something

scholarship (SKAH-lur-ship)—money given to pay for a student to follow a course of study

sumac (SOO-mak)—a spice used in Middle Eastern and Mediterranean cooking

tuition (too-ISH-uhn)—money paid to a private school or college for a student to study there

tutor (TOO-tur)—a teacher who gives private lessons to one student, or a very small group of students, at a time

❁ Glossary of Arabic Words ❁

al ustazah—professor

Allah yebarek teek—"May God bless you,"
a response to "mabrouk"

bizir—seeds

dabke—a cultural line dance in which dancers hold
hands and stamp their feet to the beat of the music

habibi—my love (to a boy)

habibti—my love (to a girl)

hajjar—rocks

mabrouk—congratulations; blessings

manaeesh—small, round bread loaves with different
toppings, such as cheese or za'atar (a spice blend)

musakhan—a dish consisting of chicken grilled with
herbs and sumac spice

salaamu alaykum—"Peace be upon you," a common
greeting

tabbouleh—an Arab salad consisting of cracked
wheat, tomatoes, parsley, and other ingredients

teta—grandma

wa alaykum al salaam—"May peace also be upon
you," the traditional response to a greeting

ABOUT THE AUTHOR

Susan Muaddi Darraj is an award-winning author of more than ten books, including two short story collections. She is an associate professor of English at Harford Community College in Bel Air, Maryland, and she also teaches creative writing at Johns Hopkins University and Fairfield University. A native Philadelphian, Susan currently lives in Baltimore. She loves books, coffee, and baseball, and she's mildly obsessed with stationery supplies.

ABOUT THE ILLUSTRATOR

Illustrator and graphic designer Ruaida Mannaa completed her undergraduate studies at the Universidad del Norte in her hometown in Colombia. She went on to pursue a Master's degree in illustration at the Savannah College of Art and Design. She grew up in a multicultural family, surrounded by different languages, loud parties, and delicious food, and she finds great inspiration for her art in culture and cultural exchange.

Farah Rocks